Little Miss Curious

by Roger Hargreaves

Little Miss Curious is a very curious
sort of person.

Just look at her house.

It's a very curious shape.

Isn't it?

Now look at her garden.

That's curious, too.

Isn't it?

Now look at Little Miss Curious.

She's rather curious looking, too.

And she also has a very curious
nature.

She wants to know the
how?
why?
and
what?
of everything.

One day, Little Miss Curious
set off for town.

"Why do doors squeak, but are not small
and furry with pink ears and long tails?"
she asked her door as she went out.

Understandably, the door didn't answer.

"Why do flowers live in beds but never sleep?" she asked the flowers in her garden.

They just smiled, knowingly.

Then she saw a worm.
"Why do worms in Nonsenseland wear
bow-ties?" she asked.

"That's for me to know and you to find
out about," said the worm, laughing.

Later, on the way to town,
Little Miss Curious met
Mr Nonsense.

Are you curious to find out
what she asked him?

Well go on then, turn over!

"I'm curious..." began Little Miss Curious, "...to know why it is that sandwiches are called sandwiches if they don't have any sand in them."

"It just so happens," said Mr Nonsense, "that this is a **sand** sandwich. I'm rather partial to sand!"

"Happy Christmas," he said.

Then Mr Nonsense ran away holding
his sandwich carefully so that the sand
didn't fall out.

Little Miss Curious eventually arrived
in town.

Did I hear you ask, "Why?"

Well, you are curious,
aren't you?

But are you as curious as
Little Miss Curious?

Little Miss Curious had gone to
town to visit the library.

"I wonder, would you be able to
help me?" she asked.

"Of course," said Mrs Page, the librarian.
"What are you looking for?"

"I'm looking for a book," began
Little Miss Curious,
"a book that will tell me
why the sky is blue..."

"...and why combs have teeth,
but can't bite,
...and why chairs have legs,
but can't play football,
...and why..."

And she went on,
and on,
and on,
until there was a very long queue
behind her, that was growing longer
by the minute.

"That's enough!" cried Mrs Page.

"NEXT PLEASE!"

"But why..." Little Miss Curious started to ask.

But without quite knowing how or why,
she suddenly found herself out in the street.

"How curious," Little Miss Curious
thought to herself.

As she walked along the street,
Little Miss Curious asked herself:
"Why is everybody giving me
such curious looks?
And why is Little Miss Careful waving
her umbrella at me?
Is it because it's going to rain?"

We don't think so, do we?

Little Miss Curious ran off.

Are you going to ask, "Why?"

Are you becoming as curious as
Little Miss Curious?

Can you guess
where she ran off to?

Neither can I.

Come back Little Miss Curious
and tell us where you're going!

You see, we're all ever so curious.

Yes, really we are!